Snail, I Love You

by
TEVAH PLATT AND WILLA THIEL

illustrated by
BECKY GROVER

Fifth Avenue Press is a locally focused and publicly owned publishing imprint of the Ann Arbor District Library. It is dedicated to supporting the local writing community by promoting the production of original fiction, non-fiction, and poetry written for children, teens, and adults.

Printed in the United States of America

First Printing, 2018

ISBN: 978-1-947989-18-4 (Hardcover);
978-1-947989-20-7 (e-book)

Fifth Avenue Press
343 S. Fifth Ave
Ann Arbor, MI 48104
fifthavenue.press

Editor
Ann Arbor District Library

Illustration
Becky Grover

Layout & Design
Ann Arbor District Library

To: _____

I love you as_____ as _____ .

Turn and grow.
Learn and know.
Spirals widen as they go.
Inching out a slime-sparkly trail,
oozing always:

I love you as curly as a snail.

The ball you throw squishes
flat when it lands.
BOINGS! off the floor
and back up to your hands.
Can you drop it and bop it?
Drop, bop, down the hall.

Because you are small,
you get pulled along FAST
over the gravel and onto the path:
Chuggita, chuggita chug
and it GLIDES!

Snail, I love you
more than wagon rides.

It feels so free to be
A thing swung on a string.
With one end fixed tight,
the other can FLING!
With a SWOOP and a LIFT
Look at me! I can fly!

Loving you feels like
a swing going high.

A million, a billion, an octodecillion!
A jillion, a willion, a wonderflazillion
Wait! Those three aren't real.
Can you make a silly one?

Snail, *I love you*
a trillion-frillion-pillion.

Ideas flash through you
in a zig-zaggy chain.
It's electric to *think*,
and to *learn*,
and *feel rain*.

Snail, I love you
like lightning
brightening
my brain.

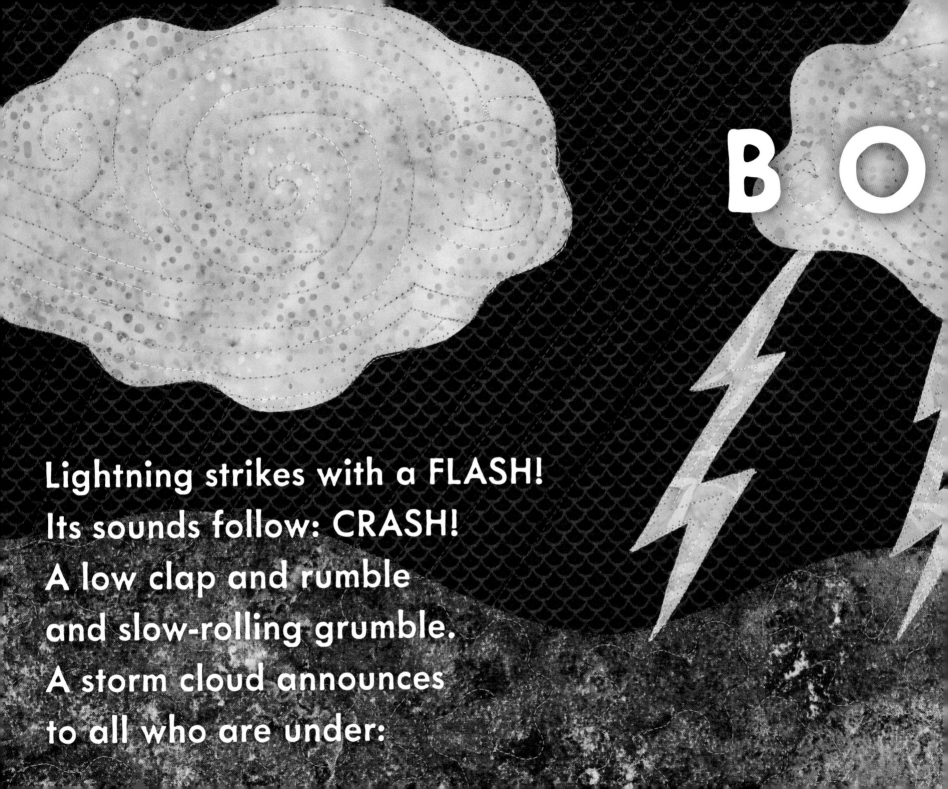

BO

Lightning strikes with a FLASH!
Its sounds follow: CRASH!
A low clap and rumble
and slow-rolling grumble.
A storm cloud announces
to all who are under:

In the woods, you feel small —
Yet a part of it all.
Rustling leaves.
Gentle chorus.

Snail, I love you
as peaceful as the forest.

Blue oceans cling tight
to the earth's every side
As the moon tugs them gently,
creating the tide.
A coconut falls to the sand.
There it stays.

Snail, I love you
as crashing as the waves.

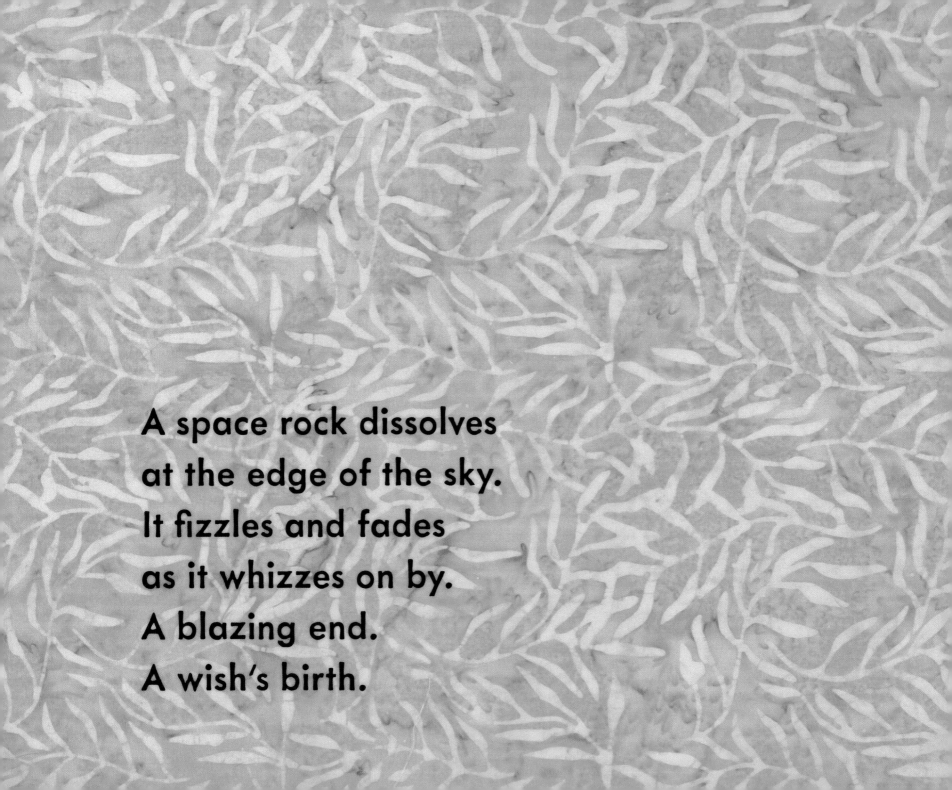

A space rock dissolves
at the edge of the sky.
It fizzles and fades
as it whizzes on by.
A blazing end.
A wish's birth.

Snail, I love you like a meteor soaring toward Earth.

Eight planets orbit around our sun.
Jupiter's the most ginormous one.
With swirling cream rivulets,
red storms of gas, and 79 moons
that each rise and pass,
and layers of air we can't inhale—

I love you as giant as Jupiter, Snail.

Our galaxy is a spiral-shaped place:
Darkness and light
held together in space.
Stars and suns in silvery spray...

Snail, I love you
as wide as the Milky Way.

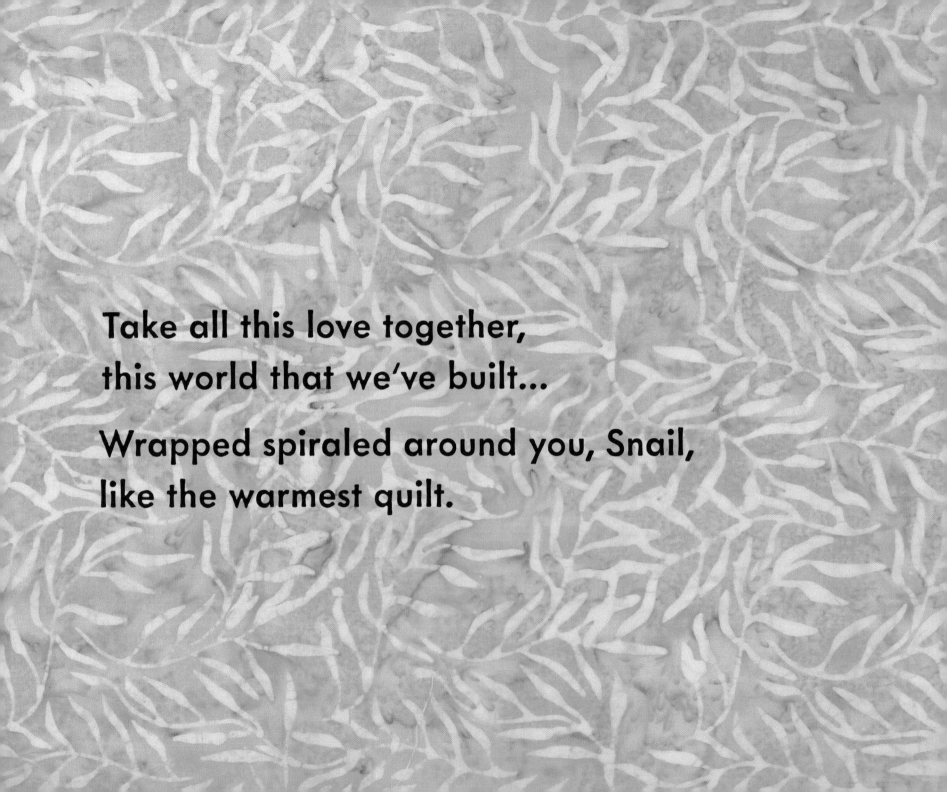

Take all this love together,
this world that we've built...

Wrapped spiraled around you, Snail,
like the warmest quilt.

About the book

This book was co-written by a mother and her daughter, who contributed each "I love you" sentence when she was between three and six years old. These words of feeling linked to concepts she was exploring and mastering while she oriented herself in the universe.

The parent-authored parts draw from the big and small worlds they joyfully investigated together. In this book about boundlessness, the authors and illustrator quietly celebrate girls as scientists and boundary breakers, and all people and animals connected by the fundamental force of love.

About the Authors

Tevah Platt is a public health researcher, science writer, and former news journalist. She likes social justice and LEGOs.

Willa Thiel worked on this book between the ages of 3-6 and is a student at Honey Creek Community School.

About the Illustrator

Becky Grover is a fiber artist whose work has traveled in shows nationally. She lives with her husband, son, and two mini-panthers (black cats). See more of her work at beckygroverdesigns. com and beckygrover.etsy.com.

Every quilted illustration in Snail, I Love You includes a snail. Their names, in order of appearance, are: Bill (cover); Dilly-Dally (ball); Lottie (wagon); Snaily McSnailface (swing); Nomi Chimmi-Bubu (hopscotch); Lea Doodledude (rain); Zayda Darwin (thunder); Morningstar (forest); Charlotte (ocean); Amify (meteor); Joe (Jupiter), and Hazel (Milky Way).

Acknowledgements

We gratefully acknowledge Fifth Avenue Press for midwifing this project: especially Sherlonya Turner for editing and brilliant coordination, "Miss Laura" Raynor for editing and for shaping Willa's preschool years with her storytelling, Tom Smith for photography, and Amanda Szot for graphic design.

The content of this book was locally inspired by the Great Oak and Touchstone Cohousing Communities, the Ann Arbor District Library, Nature Learning Community, Manzanitas Spanish Immersion Playschool, the U-M Museum of Natural History, the Ann Arbor Sewing Center, and Honey Creek Community School.

With love we also thank our families—Daniel Thiel, Dale Grover and Daniel Grover, and friends who gave us support and feedback on our work.

More than 200 people contributed to the making of *Snail, I Love You* and we thank each one of them for being a part of it. For their generous Kickstarter donations, time, advice and outpour of care we especially thank:

Amy & Malcolm
Amazing Anastasia
Anna, Oriol and Nora
Bill & Gerry
Chris Bauer
Emily Beam
Sam Boren Gonzalez
Wendy Butler Burns
Sung Choi
Kelly Clark
The Clearing
Genna Cohen
Naomi Cohen
Chandler C. Copenhaver
Matthew J. Cotter
Olas De Paul
Rhonda DeLong
Jill Dimond
KC Dixon
Jillian & Elph
Susan G. Fecteau
Carla Fine & Allen Oster

Ellen Fine & Edward Robinson
Nicolita Fisher
Erin Flynn & Sara Eilert
Francie
Erica Frantz, Cliff Williams,
Luciana & Felix
Meg Gower
Gracie
Grandma Jo, Layla & Parker
Dale & Daniel Grover
Kathryn Harris
Michael Harwood & Theo
Dorian
Anne Heaton
Dave Heppel
Lorie Honor
Becky Hoort
Dana Hughes
Noreen Hyre
Dale Jenssen
Patti Kardia
Sharon Kardia & Susan King

Mary King
Alexa Korpal
Jessica R. Kratz
Jamie, Christine, & Lottie Kucab
Theo & Clark Lane
Molly Ledermann
Maker Works
Frank, Cecilia & Helen Marotta
Katie & Ethan McAfee
John McClure
Peter Michael Miller
Maria Muller
Nana
Moira, Jeremy, Esmé &
Xanthe Nelson
Holly Painter
Pat & Rich
Brandon Patton
The Phyers Family
Jodyn Platt
Larry J. Zayda-Papa Platt
Paul Puritt

Rob, Amanda & Abby
Lea Rode
Robyn Rontal
Polly Rosenwaike & Cody Walker
Tema Sarick & Rae Nardecchia
Sayeh, Bacon, Isaac & Roya
Debbi Schaubman
Barbara M. Schrank
Mary Schroeder
Sammy and Jack Segel
Sevian & Zael & Sitara & Mark
Joe Slotnick
Joanna Snyder
Danielle Steider
Malcolm & Linda Steider
Stuart & Nancy Steider
Mary Swain
Ryan Swihart
Daniel Thiel
John, Laura & Dallas Thiel
Kay Thiel

Kristin Thiel
Martin Thiel
Katie Tilton
Irene & John Tobin
Alyssa Tool
Tommy & Mayzie
Bob Van Oosterhout
Mindy Steider Van Vynckt
Emily Warren & Duane Lee
Quentin Weir
Francesca Wong, Gary Tsifrin & Ilya Tsifrin
Margaret Wyngaard
Virginia & David
Maura Yates
Jill Zimmerman
...and all of our neighbors in the Great Oak Cohousing Community